This book
belongs to

....

To my mum and dad

FREDERICK WARNE

Published by the Penguin Group
Penguin Books Ltd, 80 Strand, London WC2R 0RL, England
Penguin Young Readers Group, 345 Hudson Street,
New York, New York 10014, U.S.A.
Penguin Books Australia Ltd, 250 Camberwell Road, Camberwell,
Victoria 3124, Australia
Canada, India, New Zealand, South Africa

1 3 5 7 9 10 8 6 4 2

ISBN: 978 07232 5921 3

Printed in Great Britain

Sweet Pea's Precious Promise

by Pippa Le Quesne

Welcome to the Flower Fairies' Garden!

Where are the fairies?
Where can we find them?
We've seen the fairy-rings
They leave behind them!

Is it a secret
No one is telling?
Why, in your garden
Surely they're dwelling!

No need for journeying,
Seeking afar:
Where there are flowers,
There fairies are!

Contents

Chapter One
Lazy Days

"Oh, you should have seen Bluebell when I came swooping through the woodland into the clearing. He was so absorbed in tending to his flowers that I took him completely by surprise. He nearly jumped out of his skin!" Snapdragon hooted with delight at the memory of his friend's astonished face peeping out from behind a nearby cherry tree.

Sweet Pea, who had been listening intently to the other Flower Fairy's story, rocked back and forth with laughter, nearly spilling her cup of nectar tea. It was always good to see Snapdragon and, as ever, he was full of amusing tales. On this particular morning he had been bursting to tell her all about the bumblebee chariot and his high-speed ride through the woods.

Without fail, Sweet Pea always enjoyed his company and although she'd only meant

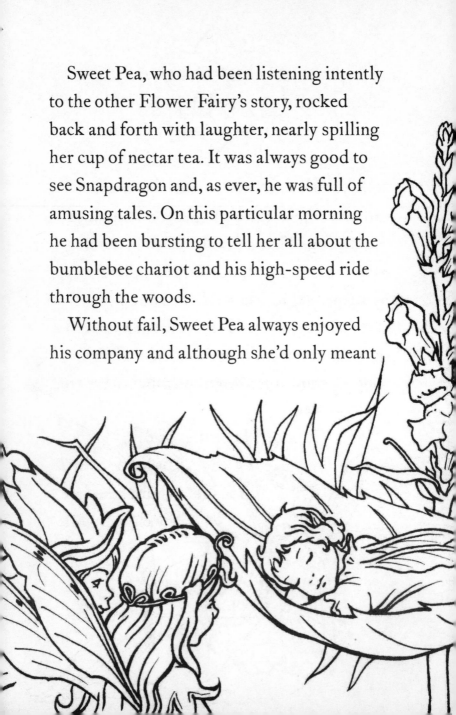

to stay for half an hour because she had to take her little sister Pea home for a nap, she'd lost all track of time. When the Garden Fairy had last glanced over, her sister, who was particularly fond of hats, had discarded her own bonnet and was trying on Snapdragon's —giggling to herself as it slipped down her face and over her eyes. And now, she was lying on her tummy with her knees up under her and her pearly wings folded against her back, looking like she was concentrating hard—as she puffed out contented little sighs of sleep.

"Oh dear," Sweet Pea said out loud. "I really meant to be home by now so that I could take care of my chores while Pea was napping. I've got a list of jobs as long as my arm and I promised Candytuft that I'd sketch out a new dress design for her ..."

"Hey, relax!" Snapdragon said cheerily. "Why don't you enjoy this bit of freedom?" He raised an eyebrow at his friend. "The hum of the bumblebees will keep Pea asleep for a good stretch and you can put your feet up."

Sweet Pea nodded in agreement and gratefully accepted a refill of nectar tea. She'd have to be super-efficient after lunch, but it was true—she hardly ever spent time

just doing *nothing*. And
she couldn't think of
many nicer places to
relax. Her friend's flowers
were some of the most
attractive in the Flower Fairies' Garden—
swirls of vibrant yellow, red and orange
petals bobbed gently on slender stalks, and
they were definitely the bumblebees'
favorite. Before you even reached
Snapdragon's patch you could hear the
pleasant drone of the furry insects, busily
burrowing for pollen.

"So tell me more about this chariot of
yours, Snap," said Sweet Pea, taking a sip of
tea. "It sounds so exciting!"

"It's marvellous," he replied, flopping
down on the grass next to her and dreamily
resting his chin in his hands. "It works
like this..."

And while Pea slept on, Snapdragon explained precisely how the chariot operated.

It was made of an extra-large, sturdy oak leaf with loops all around its edge that the clever Flower Fairy had sewn from a length of bindweed. He sat in the center of the leaf and a host of a dozen or so of the largest bumblebees would each hold a loop with their hind legs and take to the air—lifting the chariot and its passenger off the ground.

"Wow!" Sweet Pea said enthusiastically. "You must be able to go much higher and faster than we could ever hope to fly."

"Oh, yes, much!" Snapdragon replied, eagerly jumping to his feet. "And of course, I can go a really long way. Bees are strong fliers and don't get tired anywhere near as quickly as we do. Listen—I was planning to go and explore the fields this afternoon—why don't you join me?" Snap spun on the spot and then stopped in front of his friend, flinging out his arms. "Go on, you'd love it!"

Sweet Pea laughed. "It sounds fabulous —it really does. But when Pea wakes up I'll have to take her home for lunch and there are some unruly tendrils that need taming before the babies next come for a climbing lesson."

"Bring Pea with you—she'd have a ball! And the babies aren't coming today, are they? You can sort out your plants tomorrow." Snapdragon winked. "Come on, it'll be great!"

"I know. But I can't," Sweet Pea replied firmly. "Pea might tumble off and, besides, I'd be too worried that she'd get scared so I'd never be able to enjoy myself."

"OK. You know best." Snap leaned over to pick up his floppy crimson hat that was lying on the grass next to Pea. "Now, I'm off for forty winks myself. But if you change your mind, I won't be leaving for a couple of hours..." He beamed at his friend, blew her a farewell kiss and then sauntered off.

Sweet Pea sighed. It was all right for some. No doubt Snapdragon had nothing more on his mind than finding a tufty patch of grass to doze in, but she had responsibilities.

Seeing that her sister was beginning to stir, the Garden Fairy reluctantly began to gather her things. She knew that she had made the right decision but, as she searched for Pea's bonnet, she couldn't help feeling just the tiniest bit crestfallen at having to pass up the opportunity to have some fun for a change.

Chapter Two
A Stroke of Luck

Sweet Pea hummed to herself as she worked. By tucking and winding the curly tendrils of her plant around the stems that grew up the garden wall, she was creating a lattice that would hold the weight of the Flower Fairies as they made their ascent or lowered themselves back down to the ground.

The old stone wall was covered entirely in the climbing sweet peas and the hard-working Garden Fairy took pride in making sure that not only the vines provided safe hand and footholds but also the ruffled pink, purple and white blooms looked their very best. They were popular among the Flower Fairies for the wonderful scent they gave off—a mixture of honey and orange blossom—and the perfume that Sweet Pea pressed from the petals was always in demand.

"Hmm. It's been ages since I made any perfume," Sweet Pea murmured to herself. Then she wrinkled her brow. That was it, though—she always seemed to be rushed off her feet with not enough hours in the day. The little fairy sighed. *Dear old Snapdragon spends his time flying with the bees and planning adventures while my mind's always full of the next thing to take care of*, she thought.

Sweet Pea finished the loop that she was working on and, wiping her hands on her silver-green bodice, she found a nice broad leaf and sat down to think.

Everyone knows him for his bravery and his fearsome name, whereas I'm thought of as caring or helpful, she realized.

The gentle Flower Fairy loved nothing more than giving out advice or taking care of the babies, but she was beginning to wonder if it wasn't just a teensy bit boring always being the reliable one. *Am I just being silly?* she thought to herself, running through a list of her friends in her head. *Who else is like me?*

"Well, there's Tulip..." Sweet Pea said out loud. "She's wise and sought after for her

knowledge of all sorts of things. But then ...everyone thinks of her as mysterious because she comes from somewhere called Holland and originally from that

really exotic-sounding place—Persia. That's far from boring. And then there's Heather —whom the babies also love, but that's because she's a tomboy and doesn't care about her appearance, so is always tearing about involved in a game of tag. What about Honeysuckle? His plant is a climber too. But that's precisely it—rather than being the sensible one who shows everyone how to carefully lower themselves down or tells the babies not to go too high, he's notorious for being a bit of a daredevil who climbs to dizzy heights that no one else can reach."

"It's no good." Sweet Pea shook her head in dismay. "I have to face up to the fact that I'm just *too* serious. Well, I shall have to do something about that. I shall change my reputation at the very first chance I get. I'll show everyone that I know how to enjoy myself too!"

And with that, the determined Flower Fairy jumped into mid-air, spreading her wings and then soaring down to the ground where her little sister was occupied with munching on a large juicy strawberry.

* * *

"I spy, with my little eye . . ." said Sweet Pea, feeling much better after making her resolution and eating a good lunch

of delicious berries, "something beginning
with . . ." She looked around for inspiration
and caught sight of a large stone lying in the
flower bed. "S!"

"Umm," said Pea, hugely enjoying their
game, 'is it sky?"

"Nope," replied her sister.

Just then, there was a rustling, followed
by what appeared to be someone exploding
out of the flower bed. A dishevelled Flower
Fairy skidded to a halt, his arms out in front

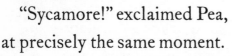

of him, concentrating
very hard on an
object that was
windmilling down
towards him.

"Got it!" he
shouted, clapping his
hands around one of his
winged seeds as it fell.

"Sycamore!" exclaimed Pea,
at precisely the same moment.

"Oh, hello there." A huge grin split the
jolly Tree Fairy's face as he caught sight of
the two amused onlookers. On his tall frame
he wore a green leaf shirt with a flamboyant
collar and irregular hemming and russet
shorts that matched his reddish-brown mop
of hair and vermillion wings.

"Want to play my game?" he asked,
helping Pea to her feet. Then he showed her

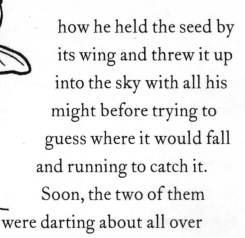

how he held the seed by
its wing and threw it up
into the sky with all his
might before trying to
guess where it would fall
and running to catch it.
Soon, the two of them
were darting about all over
the place, laughing with delight
and having a wonderful time. Sweet Pea
chuckled to herself as she put away the last
of the lunch things and decided what to do
next. She didn't have to worry about Pea for
the moment as her little sister was evidently
having fun.

Hang on a minute . . . Something suddenly
occurred to the Garden Fairy. *If Sycamore isn't
busy this afternoon . . . maybe he'd look after Pea for
me? Which would mean I could go and join Snap
on his chariot excursion!*

Such a thought was totally uncharacteristic of Sweet Pea and she felt a thrill of excitement at the possibility of doing something so impulsive. She knew that Sycamore wasn't very experienced at looking after the younger fairies but he obviously had the knack of keeping Pea entertained and she wasn't exactly a handful.

"Sycamore! Where are you? I've got a favor to ask you," she called.

"Over here, by the rose bushes," came the breathless reply.

"Right," said Sweet Pea, her mind made up. And with her stomach all aflutter, she set off to find Sycamore and Pea. Hopefully her afternoon of freedom would soon begin!

Chapter Three
Big Adventures

"Mine, mine!" shouted Pea, jumping up
in an attempt to catch the winged seed that
Sycamore had just hurled from behind
a patch of pansies. She stretched out her
fingers and stood on tiptoes, but it sailed
above her head and just out of reach, and
dropped over the rock edge of the garden.
Then, lifted by a sudden breeze, it floated
out into the middle of the lawn, where
it began its haphazard
descent.

Without a
thought for her
safety, the little
Flower Fairy

clambered down from the rocky edge, keeping an eye on the prize and scraping her knee on a rough stone as she went. 'I'll get it,' she mumbled to herself, ignoring her throbbing knee and almost tripping over her own feet in her eagerness.

Pea had been having the *best* time with Sycamore. He didn't seem to notice that she was younger than him and so had let her be just as daring—scrambling over difficult obstacles and climbing plants to retrieve the seed. It wasn't often that Sweet Pea let her wander out of her sight and as much as Pea loved her older sister, it was great to be having her very own adventure.

The climbing sweet peas lived right at the back of the garden and in the short space of the last hour, Pea had ventured further than she had ever been in her whole life. Of course she knew nearly all of the Flower

Fairies that lived in the garden and her sister
regularly took her visiting, but Pea had never
been as far as the lawn or the human house
before. She'd heard all about the humans and
knew that at all costs Flower Fairies must
be cautious and keep themselves away from
these inquisitive beings, but there was no sign
of any now and Pea didn't feel at all anxious
as she ventured away from the safety of the
flower beds.

Fully grown Flower Fairies are no taller than four inches, so Pea, who was not yet four years' old, and less than half that height, struggled to see over the tops of the blades of grass. Luckily for her, the lawn was longer than the humans usually kept it and she was well hidden, but its length meant that she couldn't be sure exactly where the seed had landed. Yet this didn't deter her in the slightest, and she continued to push her way

through the greenery in the general direction
that it had been heading.

"Pea, where are you?" came a shout from
behind her.

"Here in the grass," the little Flower Fairy
called, turning her head to see if Sycamore
was close by, still hoping that she would
be the first to reach the seed. She had been
keeping her eyes firmly on the ground, but
distracted by this exchange, she didn't notice

something lying in her path and tripped, landing roughly on her hands and knees. Picking herself up, Pea gasped when she saw what she had stumbled over.

It was a glass ball of the palest purple, attached to a beautiful silver rope that joined on to some sort of pin, which was sticking out of the earth. "What could it be?" breathed Pea, completely entranced by the object and not responding to another call from her friend, who was warning her of the dangers of the lawn.

She leaned over and picked up the ball and as she lifted it from the ground, it caught the sunlight and flashed white in her hands.

"Ooh, it's so beautiful!" she laughed, thinking how much her sister, who was very fond of pretty things, would like it.

All thoughts of Sycamore or the game left Pea's mind as she examined her treasure, imagining Sweet Pea's delight when she presented her with it. She was just wondering where in their patch they might hang it when she was jolted out of her daydream

by a hefty thud.

"Sy-sycamore?" Pea said in a small voice, as another thud shook the earth. She looked around but there was no sign of the Tree Fairy. Now the thuds were coming one after another and from more than one direction, and worse still, they were accompanied by booming voices. This could only mean one thing.

Pea began to tremble uncontrollably ... *Humans!*

* * *

"Wahoo!" cried Sweet Pea, flinging her head back so that her long auburn hair flew out in a mane behind her and she felt the cool wind rushing over her face. At that moment she felt as though she hadn't a care in the world. She was sitting beside Snap and holding on tightly to his arm to steady herself.

The bees had taken off at a moderate pace,
gently lifting the chariot over the garden
wall as their inexperienced passenger became
accustomed to the new mode of transport.
But as soon as Sweet Pea had stopped
gripping on to the sides and it was obvious
that she was beginning to enjoy herself, the
bees gathered momentum and once they'd
entered the woods, ascended to the level of
the treetops.

Snapdragon steered the chariot through
the grove of yew and wild cherry trees
and Sweet Pea marvelled at how different
everything looked from an elevated height.
The carpet of bluebells that covered the
woodland floor blurred into a sea of magenta
blue and the rabbits and squirrels playing
far below appeared to be no bigger than

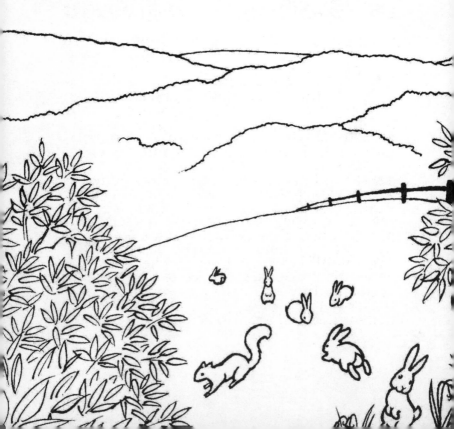

scurrying beetles.

Now they were out over the sweeping moor and, feeling a burst of confidence, the Garden Fairy had risen to her feet for a better view. She was not used to such a wide-open space or such a large scale. The endless landscape was dotted with hot pink and purple heather and wafts of the fragrant blooms were carried on the warm currents of air. She closed her eyes and drew in a deep breath.

"Let's stop for a drink with Heather," Snap suggested, turning his flushed face to his friend. "I'm sure the bees could do with a rest and I'm parched." Sweet Pea nodded vaguely in reply and he grinned when he saw how gripped she was by this new experience. "Yoo-hoo!" he called, breaking her trance. "I can hardly recognize you—you're all dishevelled and wild-looking!"

As Snapdragon pulled gently on the periwinkle threads that acted as reins, Sweet Pea glanced down at her pink skirt and white stockings and laughed. The usually pristine garment which she carefully primped into a tutu was looking sad and bedraggled and her stockings were wrinkled and sagging. But she just didn't care! Somehow, the ride on Snapdragon's chariot had cast a spell over her, making her forget all of her responsibilities and filling her with a fizzing excitement—and it felt wonderful!

Not knowing what on earth was happening
but listening to her fear, Pea threw herself
flat on the grass and lay as still as she could,
hardly daring to breathe.

After a few moments, she lifted her head
slowly off the ground and peered around
to see where the humans were. Just at that
moment a huge pair of legs came crashing
through the grass only a stone's throw from

where she lay, and it was all the Flower Fairy could do to stop herself crying out. She buried her head in her arms and screwed up her eyes, preparing herself for the worst. But nothing happened. The thumping sounds didn't stop but they appeared to have retreated to the other side of the lawn. For the moment, at least, she was safe.

Cautiously, Pea eased herself up on to her haunches and craned her neck to take another peek. It was children and there were three of them—shrieking with laughter and running about in random directions, one of them clutching a large net and swiping it through the air by its long handle.

"What are they doing?" Pea whispered in bewilderment. Then she caught sight of a pair of pale yellow wings flitting past. "Oh, a butterfly . . . poor thing, they must be trying to catch her." Forgetting her own predicament, the kind little Flower Fairy worried about the butterfly. There was nothing she could do to help, all she could hope for was that the clouded yellow would find some camouflage in among the marigolds or that the children would get bored of their game.

At that moment, she caught sight of the glass bauble that she had thrown on the ground when she first realized that she was

in danger. Still attached to its pin, it had rolled off to one side but wasn't more than a wingspan away from her and as she glimpsed it out of the corner of her eye it glinted dangerously in the sunlight. *Oh golly. If that catches their eye, I'm done for.* The little Flower Fairy shuddered at the thought. Even if she was lucky and they didn't spot her, she had no idea how she was going to get back to the safety of the rock edge of the garden without being discovered. Had Sycamore seen where she'd gone and was he on his way to help?

Just then, Pea's thoughts were interrupted by the sound of a voice, coming from the direction of the house. "Children! Come over to the step—I've got some lemonade and cake for you."

This was followed immediately by excited chatter, feet running across the lawn and then a whooshing through the air. And before Pea knew it, the net came falling out of nowhere and the frame landed heavily on the grass, bringing with it the fine mesh which, before

the surprised Flower Fairy had a chance to move, cascaded down around her. She was trapped!

* * *

"So, I thought I might wear a dress to the Autumn Ball," said Heather, handing round the dandelion and burdock juice. "And I wondered if you might help me ..." The usually bold Wild Fairy looked coyly at Sweet Pea.

"It would be my pleasure," Sweet Pea replied, tickled pink that her tomboy friend had a secret girly side. Although Heather dressed in a simple outfit of singlet and shorts and she kept her unruly blonde curls quite short, she had a creamy complexion and a very pretty face. There was no doubt that she would look beautiful in an elegant dress with some purple or hot pink heather in her hair.

Sweet Pea was just beginning to put
together a design in her head when a
large bird with a spotted chest and

white-tipped wings came swooping over
the fields towards them. Flower Fairies and
birds get along very well and this one, who
was a thrush, was one of the birds that kindly
delivered letters between the Garden Fairies
and their cousins who lived beyond the
garden boundaries.

"He must have a letter for you, Heather," commented Snap, who was lounging on a comfortable hillock, chewing a piece of nut brittle.

"How exciting," said Heather, jumping up and looking all expectant.

But the thrush wasn't carrying a parchment in his beak and after nodding politely to Heather and Snapdragon, he turned his attention to Sweet Pea. "Sycamore sent me," he said soberly. "You've got to get back to the garden—your sister is in trouble." He chirruped his message rather than talking, but all three of the Flower Fairies knew how to converse with birds and understood perfectly what he

was saying.

Sweet Pea felt herself go hot and cold all over and, when she struggled to her feet, found that her knees were weak beneath her, causing her to sit down again abruptly. She swallowed.

"Got ... to ... get back. Snapdragon—help me!" The distraught Flower Fairy looked beseechingly at her friend.

"Absolutely—let's go. The bumblebees will be refreshed by now and they'll fly like the wind. We'll be back in no time." He flashed a reassuring smile.

"Excuse me," said the bird. "Not wanting to interfere, but I'll take you. I can go much quicker than the bees."

"Of course, you're right, great idea," Snap responded, helping Sweet Pea to her feet and putting a supportive arm around her. "Now, all you have to do is to remember to hold on tight—but you'll be in very capable hands. And try not to worry; all your friends will be watching out for Pea and I've no doubt that a rescue operation is probably underway as we speak."

Sweet Pea appreciated her friend's optimism and the cheery hug that Heather gave her before she climbed on to the thrush's back, but she felt sick with dread and couldn't muster a reply or even a simple farewell. All she could think of was how awful she was for having left poor Pea in order to indulge some silly dream, and how her precious little sister was probably now in some grave danger because of her. If something terrible happened ... Sweet Pea couldn't even finish this thought. She patted the thrush to let him know that she was ready and concentrated all her being on getting back to the garden as fast as possible. She would do *whatever* it took to put things right.

Chapter Five
A Daring Plan

"Where is she, where is she?" Sweet Pea cried, practically hurling herself at Guelder Rose. It had taken the thrush no time at all to fly from the fields to the Flower Fairies' Garden, but to Sweet Pea it had felt like the longest few minutes of her life. As soon as the bird had landed she'd rushed off as fast as her legs could carry her.

There was no sign of Sycamore but when Sweet Pea pushed her way through a cluster of lupins, she'd caught sight of Guelder Rose and Apple Blossom standing on one of the craggy stones at the front of the garden's edge, peering out in the direction of the lawn.

Now, she was firing questions at the two Flower Fairies, barely drawing breath or giving them time to provide her with the answers. "Is Pea all right? What happened? Where is she? Have the humans got her? And where *is* Sycamore?"

Guelder Rose, who was one of the gentlest and most softly spoken fairies, calmly took Sweet Pea's hands in hers and said, "It's all right. Sycamore has got it all under control. Now, can you see that net lying in the grass? Well, Pea is trapped under there—" Then noticing the distress on her friend's face, she hurried on with her explanation. "There's no reason to worry—she's not hurt or frightened and she knows that help is on its way. And the humans don't know she's there—they're sitting on the step by the house having

50

something to eat. See?"

"Oh, I must get to her immediately," sobbed Sweet Pea, pulling away from Guelder Rose. Unable to let her eyes linger on the terrifying net or the children, who, thankfully, were still occupied with their cake, all she wanted to do was follow her instincts and get to her sister fast.

"Listen," continued Guelder Rose, "I know this must be unbearably hard for you, but if you rush out there

you'll not only risk getting yourself spotted but you'll draw attention to Pea too. You've got to trust Sycamore—he's got a rescue plan all sorted. And before you know it, Pea will be back here with you, safe and sound."

Apple Blossom nodded in agreement, a genuine look of concern and sympathy on her heart-shaped face. Both of the Tree Fairies had little sisters and so Sweet Pea knew that they understood precisely how she was feeling. Although it didn't make her feel better, it helped a bit. And knowing that they'd never do anything to compromise Pea's safety, she reluctantly let them lead her back to the lupins where they'd be hidden from view but would still be able to see everything that went on.

* * *

"Ready?" whispered Sycamore.
"Ready!" Lily-of-the-Valley nodded,

producing a small folded handkerchief from
the pocket of her smock.

"Right. Well, as soon as you've released
the fairy dust we'll set off," Sycamore said.
"Good luck!"

The other Flower Fairies that were
huddled with them in the clump of
dandelions murmured their best wishes and

Lily smiled gratefully before hitching up her white dress in one hand and striding away. A cluster of her flowers grew in a bed at the edge of the lawn, furthest from the house. They consisted of small white bells arranged on short delicate stems which swayed in the wind, creating a tinkling sound perfectly audible to the fairies but not usually heard by humans. When Lily reached them she wasted no time in unfolding the handkerchief that she had shown to Sycamore, and, shaking it out over the plants, she murmured, "Fairy dust, fairy dust, do me proud. Make my bells sparkle and ring out loud."

When the tiny particles of ground-up pollen first settled, they covered each dainty flower with a thin layer of almost invisible dust, but as soon as the Flower Fairy had cast her spell they began to dance and

sparkle like hundreds of miniature fireflies.
In turn, the flowers came to life and started
to shake and ring, each one producing a
chiming sound that was loud enough to alert
the humans to the magical activity taking
place in their garden.

"Wow! Look at that!" one of the girls
shouted, charging across the grass.

As Lily vanished into a neighbouring crop of forget-me-nots, she saw the rescue party take to the air. "Be careful!" she whispered after them.

Sycamore, Cornflower, Dandelion and Grape Hyacinth made up the group of Flower Fairies that nimbly flew the short distance to where Pea was trapped. The

courageous little Flower Fairy, taking care
not to entangle herself further in the mesh,
had crawled to the edge of the net and was
eagerly awaiting her friends' arrival.

"There's not a moment to lose," instructed
Sycamore, winking reassuringly at Pea. "On
the count of three, we lift. Ready?" Then,
leading by example and placing his hands

under the thick wooden hoop, he took a deep breath and counted, "One, two, THREE!"

The four Flower Fairies heaved with all their might and succeeded in lifting the net just far enough off the ground for Pea to wriggle out on her tummy. They were about to let it drop to the ground when there was an urgent cry from the liberated prisoner.

"Wait!" said Pea—lunging back under and grabbing something with both hands before rolling out on to the grass.

Unable to take the weight of the net any

longer and seeing that the young Flower
Fairy was out of range, the rescuers let the
heavy object slip from their grasp.

"Phew!" exclaimed Dandelion, beaming.
"We did it!"

"Er, not quite," responded Sycamore,
a note of alarm in his voice. "Lily's fairy
dust is beginning to fade and as soon as the
humans lose interest, we're done for!"

Sweet Pea wasn't sure if she could stand
much more of this emotional rollercoaster.
She had gone from blind panic to uncertain

hope, and then to complete rapture when her sister finally emerged from the net. A wave of sweet relief had washed over her at the sight of Pea—rumpled, but very much still in one piece. Yet, when she checked on the children gathered around the lily-of-the-valleys, Sweet Pea noticed that the flowers were merely glimmering now and that their ringing was becoming more and more faint with every second. The humans were still totally bewitched by the extraordinary spectacle and were discussing it with no less enthusiasm, but she was sure that it was only a matter of time before one of them ran back to the house to fetch their mother. The sight of five real-life fairies flying across the lawn would far outshine the chiming flowers and with a net to hand, Flower Fairyland would be doomed.

Sweet Pea felt her knees weaken again and

was glad when Guelder Rose thoughtfully slipped an arm around her. "They'll think of something," she said encouragingly. "You'll see."

"Look," Apple Blossom cut in. "It looks like they're crawling."

All at once, the rescue party had dropped to their knees and then completely out of sight. It seemed as if they were lying down,

but then—just visible from their lookout—
the blades of grass began to part ever so
slightly at the top in a rippling effect that was
moving towards the rock edge of the garden.
It was as though something or *some bodies*
were making their way towards them, slowly
but surely.

"They must be crawling!" exclaimed
Guelder. "I told you they'd come up with a
plan." And the petite Flower Fairy whirled
round in delight, causing her white layered

skirt to fan out around her.

"But she's so little," said Sweet Pea, tears welling in her eyes. "*Nothing* like this has ever happened to her before. And I know how capable the boys are, but I'm worried about Pea. She must be beside herself and if she goes to pieces, I'm the only one that will be able to calm her down."

Sweetpea took a deep breath and flexed her pretty wings. If Pea wasn't back in one minute she was going to have to launch a rescue mission all of her own . . .

Chapter Six
A Special Promise

"There," said Pea decisively. "It looks perfect just there."

Sweet Pea tapped the pin into the wall with a pebble and stood back to admire her handiwork. The sun had nearly set and the milky light of dusk didn't show off the glass bauble at its best, but as it swung back and forth from the silver rope, flickers of pink and purple from the surrounding sweet peas danced across its surface. It was beautiful!

The older Flower Fairy allowed herself a chuckle.

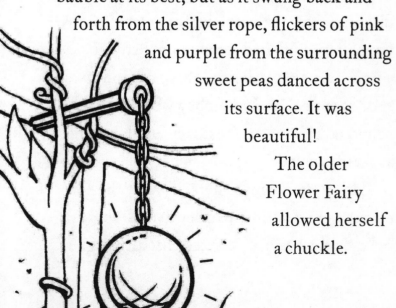

It had been the most eventful day of her life—with some of the best moments and definitely some of the worst.

Earlier on, just as she had been ready to launch herself off on her desperate mission to retrieve Pea, Cornflower had poked his head up over the side of the garden, and moments later her sister's beaming face appeared. Sweet Pea had been so relieved, and Pea had been so proud of her own bravery, that all feelings of worry or anger just seemed to dissolve away in the celebratory atmosphere. Grape Hyacinth had insisted on them all coming for a revitalizing cup of tea and a spot of supper and soon they were all sitting round talking ten to the dozen and laughing at their escapade.

Taking a moment to herself while the others were chatting in order to mull things over, Sweet Pea had realized that although

Pea had been in terrible danger, she could just have easily got into a similar sticky situation in *her* care. Plus, it was the quick-thinking and nerve of the others, not her, that had saved the day. It would do her good to remember that if there were Flower Fairies about Pea would always be looked after. And she wasn't sure she'd be able to forget that marvellous taste of freedom that she'd experienced flying over the fields on the bumblebee chariot.

Sweet Pea took one last glance at Pea's gift—that Sycamore had identified as a human earring—and then turned round to lift up her sister in an embrace. "I'm *so* glad to be home and to have you safely with me. But," she said, catching the look that Pea gave her, "I promise that from now on, I won't be so protective and I will make sure that there's plenty of time every day for us to enjoy ourselves. And to show you that I mean it, we'll go over and see Snapdragon first thing tomorrow and arrange for him to take us *both* on a chariot ride just as soon as he can."

"I love you!" cried Pea with joy. "You're the best sister in the world."

"I love you too," said Sweet Pea, burying her face in her sister's hair, all dusty and tangled from her adventure. Then, once more catching a glimpse of the earring dangling from the wall, she made an oath to herself—every time she caught sight of the jewel it would serve as a reminder

of the lesson she had learned that day. And
no matter how busy she was, she would
always keep her promise to precious Pea.

Visit our Flower Fairies website at:

www.flowerfairies.com

There are lots of fun Flower Fairy games and activities for you to play, plus you can find out more about all your favorite fairy friends!

Log onto the Flower Fairies Friendship Ring

Visit the Flower Fairies website to sign up for the new Flower Fairies Friendship Ring!

★ No membership fee
★ News and updates
★ Every new friend receives a special gift!
(while supplies last)